High-Frequency READERS™

THE BAND

Written by Nancy Leber
Illustrated by Linda Helton

Scholastic Inc.
New York   Toronto   London   Auckland   Sydney
Mexico City   New Delhi   Hong Kong

ISBN 0-439-13192-8

12 11 10 9   5/0
Printed in China   62

Can you see the guitar?

Can you see the drum?

Can you see the horn?

Can you see the harmonica?

Can you see the triangle?

Can you see the kazoo?

Can you see the band?